Published by Foxey World Publishing
Division of The Friends of Rick Daniels Inc.
731 Jefferson ST NW Washington, DC 20011 USA
(202) 722-0502 / www.thefriendsofrickdaniels.com

Cover design by Cecille Kaye Gumadan
Illustrations by Denis Prouix

Published in the United States of America
ISBN: 978-0-692-34716-4
Juvenile Fiction / Social Issues / Bullying

ACKNOWLEDGEMENTS

Being bullied has dramatically changed my life, and I would like to thank all the hospitals, doctors, therapists, Social workers, case managers, close friends and neighbors that have given me the strength to go on through these difficult times.

I would like to also give a special thanks to The National

Suicide Prevention Lifeline for being there for me late at night when I had no one else to call.

To the hundreds of kids that send me emails from all over the world thanking me for bringing awareness about bullying and suicide prevention.

To Pixie and Dixie and all the other squirrels and birds that I feed on a daily basis. On my worst days I only wish you could understand the joy it brings me when feeding you.

To my illustrator Denis Proulx. Thank you for bringing my book to life.

Preface

Ever since I was a very young child I was teased and made fun of because I could not read or write. As the years grew so did the teasing and the making fun of me. Nowadays it's called bullying. Being teased and made fun of by classmates, coworkers, stranger, and friends were not the worst times in my life. The worst times were my senior year's right after my mom died. I was bullied my members of my family, sending me on a roller coaster ride of depression and PTSD. When I first got the idea to write a book about bullying, instead of writing about current events, I wanted to reach out to children at the age when I first experienced being bullied. I strongly believe that the earlier a child learns that bullying can have serious consequences, the less likely they are to bully people as they get older.

Little Remy does not like to get up in the morning to go to school.

Every morning Little Remy's mom has to *pull* and *pull* and *pull* him out of bed to get him ready for school.

Little Remy tells his mom, "I don't wanna to go school."

"Why don't you want to go to school?"

"Because the kids tease and make fun of me."

"Why do the kids tease and make fun of you?"

"Because I can't read or write."

"What do the kids say to you?"

"They say mean things to me, like, 'you're stupid,' and 'dummy,' and then they push me!

"Oh, so they are bullying you."

"Mom, what's bullying?"

"When people are mean to you or call you bad names, that's called bullying."

"But that's not nice!"

"You're so right. Bullying is not a good thing."

"Mom, then why do people bully other people?"

"They do it for all the wrong reasons. It could be the color of your skin, where you are from, the clothes you wear, or even a disability."

"Mom why can't I read and write?"

"You have a learning disability."

"Mom what's a learning disability?"

"When you were younger you were very sick and that's why you have trouble reading and writing."

"Mom, is that why the kids at school bully me?"

"Unfortunately yes."

"Mom, is there any way to stop people from bullying other people?"

"It won't be easy but we can try."

"Don't you worry about bullying right now, you just get ready for school or you'll be late."

So Little Remy's mom decides to do something about the bullying at Little Remy's school.

Later that day Little Remy's mom went to his school to see what she could do about the bullying at Little Remy's school.

Little Remy's mom met with the school's principal and they decided to protest and start a campaign to drive bullying out of Little Remy's school.

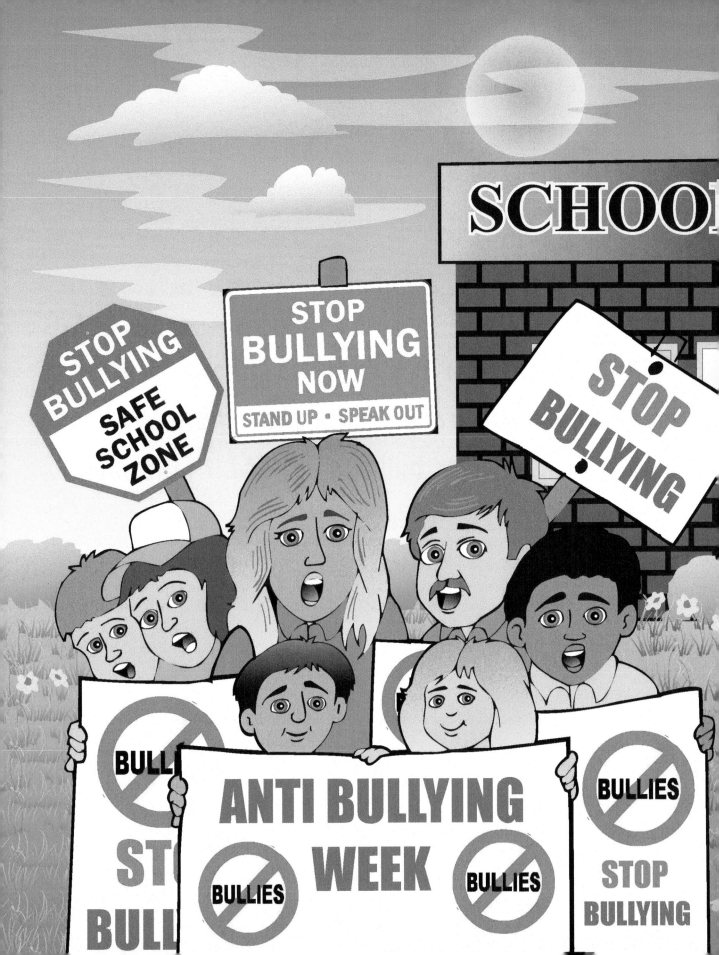

Everyone got involved! The anti-bullying campaign was a success!

They drove all the bullies out of Little Remy's school!

Little Remy was now a hero! His mom's campaign got rid of all the bullies at Little Remy's school, and now school was safe for all.

The End

You can follow the life of Little Remy as he struggles with being bullied, having a learning disability, and other shocking events that come to life for a little boy who can't read or write in my next two books.

A Word About The Author

Rick Daniels is 64 years old and growing up in DC public schools with a learning disability made it very difficult for him. He was passed on from grade to grade and kept back twice. When he entered the 10th grade he was 18 years old and DC public schools are not obligated to keep you in day school once you turn 18, so he left. Although he could not read or write he was quite creative and fashion was his thing. Rick moved to New York City and took evening classes in fashion design at New York's Fashion Institute of Technology. He never graduated from FIT because of his learning disability, but he learned enough to open his own business, Foxey World Shirts. He designed shirts for dozens of celebrities and his shirts were sold in boutiques and department stores nationwide, his shirts were also featured in fashion magazine worldwide. Rick also worked at Avis Rent a Car. While working at Avis, Rick received many awards for superior customer service. In 2001 he went on to get his GED and took some college courses. In 2003 he attended the Washington Literary Council for additional help with his learning disability. Rick still struggles with reading and writing, but he hope his books will both educate and entertain his readers.

A WORD TO ADULTS

BULLYING: Bullying is an activity of repeated and aggressive behavior intended to hurt another person physically, mentally, or emotionally. People bully other people to gain power over that person for several reasons. Maybe they were bullied themselves and like the feeling it give them to see someone else suffering as they did. Or maybe it make them feel like a big shot at school.

When it comes to bullying parents and teachers are sometimes the last to know. Kids that get bulled are usually too afraid to talk to an adult about it because of retaliation from the bully or bullies. Bullies are usually at their best when there is no one around to catch them in the act; before or after school and during lunch period.

WARNING SIGNS: If you think your child may be a victim of being bullied, (adapted from the US Department of Health & Human Services guide) your child may exhibit some of the following signs:

- Comes home with dirty, torn, or wet clothes or 'loses" things without being able to explain what happened.
- Has unexplained bruises, cuts and scratches, or other injuries.
- Loses interest in school and gets poor grades.
- Does not bring friends home or visit with friends after school.
- Seems afraid or refuses to go to school.
- Takes an" illogical" route to school.
- Seems unhappy, downhearted, depressed or moody, has sudden outbursts of anger.
- Eats poorly or complains of headaches or stomachaches.

- Sleeps poorly, cries out in his sleep or has nightmares.
- Asks for extra money (because a bully is demanding it.)

LEARNING DISABILITY: Children with a learning disability or disorder are not always a true learning disability. In some cases that child may have just gotten behind and needs help from a teacher or tutor, but if not caught in time then it can become a problem. Either way it's up to the teachers and parents to recognize that there is a problem. Children with a learning disability can and do succeed.

LEAD POISONING: According to Daniel J. DeNoon, senior medical writer for webMD, lead poisoning at levels that do not cause immediate symptoms can permanently damage kid's brains before their second birthday. Children are particularly susceptible to lead poisoning. They are, of course more likely than older children to put lead-contaminated hands or toys or paint chips in their mouths. According to health kid's.org; Children with a history of 'pica" a disorder characterized by persistent and compulsive cravings to eat non-food items like dirt, paint chips or clay are also at risk of lead poisoning. According to the CDC about 310,000 American kids' 1 to 5 years old have levels of lead in their blood. Lead Poisoning may affect a child's impairments in language fluency or communication, memory problems, trouble paying attention, and lack of concentration.

If you think you child is being bullied, or do you have a child with a learning disability. Or maybe you are a parent that's just not sure what to do. Then visit some of the sites I have listed on the next page:

- The Bully Project: 18 West 27 ST 2nd Floor New York, NY 10001 (212) 725-1220 http://www.thebullyproject.com

- Stop bulling.gov http://www.stopbullying.gov

- The Wilson Reading System: 47 Old Webster Road Oxford MA 01540 (800) 899-8454 or 368-2399 http://www.wilsonlanguage.com

- Pacer Center Champions for Children with Disabilities Pacer Center, Inc. 8161 Normandale, Blvd. Bloomington, MN 55437 (800) 537-2237 or (952) 838-9000-900: http://www.pacer.org/contactpacer.asp.

- WebMD Children's Health Center: hhttp://webmd.com: kid's Healthe: http://kidshealthe.org.

- Center for Disease and Control Prevention: http://www.cdc.gov.

KEY WORDS:

Bullying

Disability

Stupid

Dummy

Push me

CPSIA information can be obtained
at www.ICGtesting.com
Printed in the USA
BVOW07s0619020916

460825BV00006B/7/P